# Misplaced in Space

by
**Justin Spelvin**

illustrated by
**Dave Aikins**

SCHOLASTIC INC.

New York  Toronto  London  Auckland  Sydney
Mexico City  New Delhi  Hong Kong  Buenos Aires

The Space Explorers were on a mission. They were going to be the first explorers to see the Cosmic Comet. "Man your stations, team. It's time to blast off from the spaceport," said Commander Tasha.

"Why are you giving the commands?" asked Pilot Pablo.

"I'm the COMMAND-er," explained Tasha. "It's in my title."

"But I fly the ship," said Pilot Pablo.

"Uh, have either of you seen the space map?" First Mate Austin asked.

Just then Commander Tasha spotted another ship getting ready for takeoff. "If we don't hurry up, they'll beat us to the comet!" she shouted.

"What about our space map?" asked First Mate Austin.

"Right, right," Commander Tasha answered distractedly. "The comet's path is marked on our space map."

"WAIT!" shouted Austin. "That isn't what I—"

"Fire the engines, Pilot Pablo!" the commander ordered.
"Whatever you say," grumbled Pilot Pablo. He hit the light
speed button. The ship zoomed away.

When the ship finally slowed down, the team found themselves in the middle of a space cloud!

"This isn't the right spot," said Pilot Pablo. "Let's look at the map."

First Mate Austin shook his head. "We can't *find* the map."

"Really? I wish I had known that before we left," Commander Tasha said.

"Don't worry. I'll just reverse our course and take us back to the spaceport," suggested Pilot Pablo.

"Hey, I'm the commander here!" responded Tasha.

Just then the other ship from the spaceport flew into view. "They must be following us because they want to see the Cosmic Comet, too. Quick! Set a course for Gamma Alpha Alpha!" ordered the commander.

"But we don't know—," First Mate Austin started to say.

"Don't you want to get to the Cosmic Comet first?" Commander Tasha asked.

Pilot Pablo sighed and pushed the light speed button.

When the ship slowed down, though, the comet was nowhere to be seen.

"This isn't right," said Commander Tasha.

"I told you we should have gone back," said Pilot Pablo.

"But then we wouldn't be the first ones to reach the comet," Tasha pointed out.

First Mate Austin had something else to say: "ASTEROIDS!"

Giant space rocks were coming
at them from every direction.

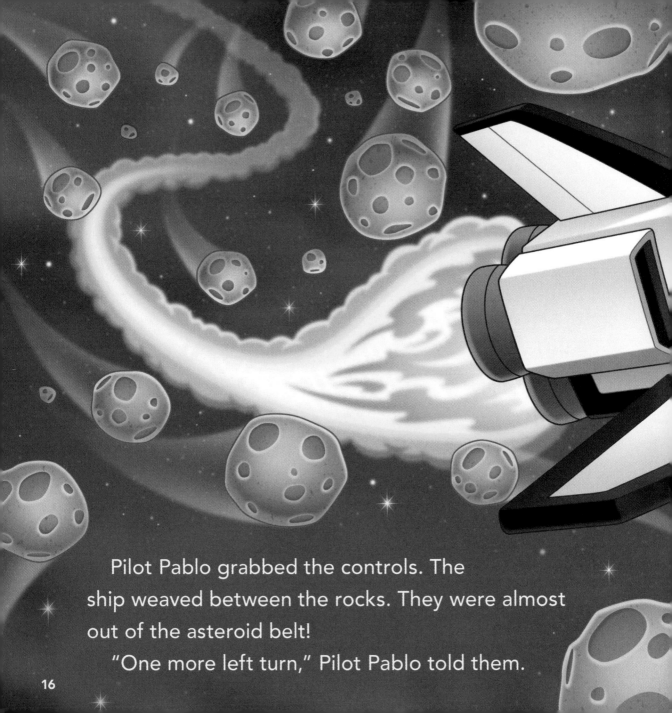

Pilot Pablo grabbed the controls. The
ship weaved between the rocks. They were almost
out of the asteroid belt!

"One more left turn," Pilot Pablo told them.

"No, a right turn!" said Commander Tasha.

"It's a left. Right, First Mate Austin?" asked the pilot.

"Right," Austin agreed. "I mean—"

But Pilot Pablo turned right and SMASH! An asteroid struck the ship's wing.

Sirens blared. Lights flashed. And everyone shouted at the same time.

"We need to make repairs right now!" shouted the commander.

"We should land on that moon!" shouted the pilot.

"Wait! We don't have the parts we need!" shouted the first mate.

But neither the pilot nor the commander listened to Austin.

"Okay, let's fix the ship!" said Commander Tasha when they had landed.

"We don't have the parts we need," repeated First Mate Austin.

"Why didn't you say that?" asked the commander.

"I *did*!" yelled First Mate Austin. "You weren't listening and now we're stuck."

"I knew I should have been in charge," Pilot Pablo said.

First Mate Austin had heard enough! "Who cares who's in charge if we aren't listening to each other?"

Pilot Pablo and Commander Tasha were quiet for a moment.

"He's right," the pilot said.

"We need a plan," said the commander. "Okay, who has some ideas? I'm listening."

"If we could find some scrap metal we could fix the wing," said Pilot Pablo.

"Hey, there's that other ship again!" said First Mate Austin. "Maybe we could ask them for help."

23

The other ship landed. Space Explorers Tyrone and Uniqua were inside!

"You guys are hard to catch!" Space Explorer Uniqua exclaimed. "We have something of yours."

"You left your map at the spaceport," said Space Explorer Tyrone.

Space Explorers Uniqua and Tyrone helped Pablo and Tasha fix their ship.

Meanwhile, First Mate Austin checked the space map. "Look, everyone!" he said. "The Cosmic Comet isn't far away."

They agreed to go together.

The Cosmic Comet was beautiful!

"Wow! Look out of the left window," said Commander Tasha.

"Look out of the right window," said Pilot Pablo at the same time.

They looked at each other, smiled, and looked out
of *both* windows.

And everyone had a terrific view.

# Nick Jr. Play-to-Learn™ Fundamentals
## Skills every child needs, in stories every child will love!

**colors + shapes**
Recognizing and identifying basic shapes and colors in the context of a story.

**emotions**
Learning to identify and understand a wide range of emotions, such as happy, sad, and excited.

**imagination**
Fostering creative thinking skills through role-play and make-believe.

**mathematics**
Recognizing early mathematics in the world around us, such as patterns, shapes, numbers, and sequences.

**music + movement**
Celebrating the sounds and rhythms of music and dance.

**physical**
Building coordination and confidence through physical activity and play.

**problem solving**
Using critical thinking skills, such as observing, listening, and following directions, to make predictions and solve problems.

**reading + language**
Developing a lifelong love of reading through high interest stories and characters.

**science**
Fostering curiosity and an interest in the natural world around us.

**social skills + cultural diversity**
Developing respect for others as unique, interesting people.